MW00943601

THE GREAT UFO FRAME-UP

RANDY HORTON

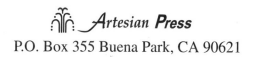

Artesian Press
P.O. Box 355 Buena Park, CA 90621

Take Ten Books
Adventure

Other Take Ten Themes:
Mystery
Sports
Disaster
Chillers
Thrillers
Fantasy

Project Editor:Liz Parker
Cover Illustrator:Marjorie Taylor
Cover Designer: Tony Amaro
Text Illustrator:Fujiko Miller
©2000 Artesian Press

 *Artesian Press*

ISBN 1-58659012-X

Chapter 1

Picture the universe. It's larger than you can imagine, so don't be upset if you can't do it justice. The universe is big, and even when you think of big, it's bigger than that. We have billions of galaxies in our universe, and each galaxy is made up of just as many stars. Most of those stars have at least a few planets swirling around them. No one knows yet how many of those planets support life, but one thing is certain: The most boring astronomy class in the entire universe is Mr. Bledso's Astronomy 101, on the second floor of Spiro Agnew Junior High School, room 203, Julius County, California, Earth. Jed Fisk realized this fact on the second day of class. He'd missed the first day or he would have realized it then.

Jed was tall and a little too thin. He was brown. He had brown hair, brown eyes, a dark suntan, and at the moment, a very dark picture of life. Jed sat in the back row of room 203, next to the window, watching cars speed up onto the freeway from the Main Street on-ramp. If you can imagine how boring this was, you have some idea what Astronomy 101 was like. Mr. Bledso, who taught the class, was old and bald; he looked like a wax statue. He had a stutter, and when he wasn't stuttering, he was mumbling. Jed used to like astronomy, but in just under fifty minutes his entire outlook had changed. Jed walked out of room 203 hating astronomy. In fact, he hated the universe. He hated each galaxy, every star, and any planets that might be circling around them. His friend, Pal Linsky, agreed.

"I wanted to hear about aliens," Pal said. "All he talked about was Aristotle. Who cares about a bunch of Greeks?" Pal was fat, blond, cross-eyed, and nervous.

Jed followed Pal downstairs out to the courtyard. "Bledso was mumbling so much I thought his lecture was in Greek."

It was lunch time. Jed sat with Pal on a low concrete wall, watching cheerleaders practice their moves. They had an hour to sulk over the horrors of modern education.

"Besides," said Pal, "Aristotle got it all wrong. He thought Earth was the center of the universe. Why even bother with that guy?"

"It's a sad day," said Jed. "School just started, and I'm already waiting for summer." He pictured the weeks that lay ahead of him, each one containing five classes of Astronomy 101. Four weeks a month, and four months in the semester. Jed knew that he would go crazy.

"There's only one way we're going to get out of this," Pal said. Jed was watching the cheerleaders, so he pretended not to listen.

"I said," said Pal, "there's only one way we're going to get out of this mess!"

"You don't have to yell. How?"

"Aliens." Pal smiled confidently. "If aliens take us away in a spaceship we'd miss the whole semester."

"That's it? That's how we get out of astronomy class?" Jed stared at his friend and waited for an explanation. Pal read too much science fiction. Most everybody at school thought he was a bit of a dork. In fact, he *was* a bit of a dork, but Jed knew Pal wouldn't say something so stupid without a reason.

"Haven't you been watching the news?" Pal said. "Last week two people saw unidentified lights in the sky near

the state park."

"So?" Jed wished he hadn't spent all of his lunch money on video games, he was hungry, and he wasn't in the mood for imaginary escapes from the cold, hard reality of Spiro Agnew Junior High School.

"So," Pal said, "we go camping in the park, we make mysterious lights of our own, we leave evidence of a space-ship, and we spend the rest of the se-mester living in my uncle's cabin down by Kroger's Lake. My uncle hasn't used his cabin in over a year. He gained too much weight; all he does now is watch TV. But we'd need some proof when we get back," said Pal, "so I guess it wouldn't work."

"No," said Jed. "We'll just find some weird junk and say it's from the space ship."

"Well..." Pal was nervous. "It's prob-ably not a good idea. My parents would worry if I didn't come home for four months." Pal always came up with the ideas, but he never wanted to go through with them. Without Jed, Pal was just a dreamer. This was the main reason Pal's parents told him to stay away from Jed.

Jed stood and faced him. "Are you going to chicken out on me?"

"Well, you know … my mom's been sick. What happens when we get back?"

"We'll be famous!" Jed pointed to the cheerleaders jumping in the air and screaming out letters of the alphabet. "Not one of those females knows you exist. And if any one of them did, she wouldn't admit it. If aliens take us away on a spaceship for four months, you and I will go on the local news. We can get dates! Even ugly and stupid people get dates if they're famous. Don't you know anything?"

"But what if we get caught?"

"Get caught?" Jed shook his head in

disgust, "Did that worry John Dillinger? or Richard Nixon? or King Kong? Where would America be today if our ancestors had worried about being caught? We'd be a colony of England. They still have kings and queens in England. Are you going to be afraid all your life? Are you going to do exactly what everyone tells you to do? Or are you going to claim some self-respect and help me create a fake alien kidnapping?"

Pal searched for an argument, but the cheerleaders seemed to have made him forget everything. He pictured himself locked in a kiss with Amy Shroeden, his next-door neighbor and the most beautiful girl he had ever seen. Yes, she was saying, I never realized how attractive you were—until those aliens kidnapped you.

"Well," Pal nodded, looking down, "it looks like we're about to be kidnapped."

On the field, beautiful young women in yellow and red leaped into the air, cheering wildly. Jed pictured himself on television, calmly describing the aliens. All the universe seemed to smile down upon him.

Chapter 2

There was no time to lose. Jed slept over at Pal's house that night. They sat around the Linsky's kitchen table outlining their Master Plan. The rest of Pal's family was in the den, watching a made-for-television movie made almost entirely of car chases, explosions, and commercials. "They'll never be able to hear us," said Pal. "My mom is deaf in one ear, so they crank up the volume."

"We have to do this right," Jed said. "We can't get caught or they'll send us off to detention for the rest of the year."

"Right," said Pal, "Here's the plan: First we find out how to get people's attention with our fake UFO. Second, we have to find some space junk to leave around. It has to look weird and like it's from the future. Third, we bring food and a couple of astronomy books so we can make up a good story. Then we hike out to my uncle's cabin, and we're done!"

"Done!" said Jed. The plan was simple. It was direct. He couldn't imagine anything possibly going wrong. "So, you have some cold pepperoni pizza in the refrigerator? This is making me hungry."

Pal shook his head. "My mom's a vegetarian, too. If we want any meat we have to go down the street to the Burger'n'Joy."

Jed clapped his chubby friend on the shoulder. "Well, cheer up, Pal. I've got five bucks; let's celebrate. On the way I'll tell you exactly how we're going to fake this little UFO." Jed wasn't sure about everything himself, but he had faith that as he talked, the details would work themselves out

In fact, nothing worked out. Jed heard somewhere that tiny hot-air balloons could be made with candles and tissue paper. He tried this the next day, but the tissue caught on fire. He used plastic lunch bags next, but they were too heavy, and they melted. The whole idea was a failure.

Jed sat alone in the Burger'n'Joy. His balloon experiments had all been disasters. He was feeling like a disaster himself. He was drinking a chocolate shake and staring at the greasiest french fries in the known galaxy.

Feeling desperate, Jed wadded the fries up into a ball and watched sadly as the oil dripped out onto his napkin. Then, from the back of the Burger'n'Joy he heard the sound of laughing children. It was a birthday party for little Elizabeth Herndon who lived down by the sewage treatment plant. Jed squeezed his fries even harder. Who cares, he thought, about a dumb birthday party—a bunch of stupid kids, cake, ice cream, a man in a clown suit … and helium balloons!

Balloons! Right there against the far wall, a man in a cotton polka-dotted jumper stood next to a small cannister of helium, filling up balloons!

Jed had to find a way to borrow the clown's helium tank. He weaved through the kids, dodging chunks of flying birthday cake, and stood next to the clown.

"My name's Jed," he said.

"I'm Lucky the Birthday Clown," said the man. He had a New York accent and didn't seem particularly friendly. He wore a bright orange wig and his face was covered in white make-up. "You want a balloon or what?"

"I want to rent your tank this weekend," said Jed. "How much would it cost?"

Lucky shook his head and laughed. "Rule number one, kid: A clown never gets separated from his tank. It's the first thing they teach you in clown school." He wiped the make-up from his lips onto a sleeve. "Help the little girl behind you with a balloon, would you? I'm going to light up a smoke while their mom is in the toilet." Lucky fished through his pocket for a pack of cigarettes.

"I want a red one!" Little Elizabeth Herndon punched Jed in the arm.

"Aren't these kids a pain?" Lucky coughed and put out his cigarette. "These things are killing me. Never start smoking, kid. Tomorrow I quit."

"Look," Jed was growing annoyed with the clown's attitude. "I just want to borrow your tank on Saturday night. I'll bring it back Sunday. I have money."

"Money, huh…" Lucky scratched his stubbly chin. "How many balloons do you want filled?"

Jed picked a number at random. "Fifty."

"Fifty! That's three-quarters of the

tank. Fifty balloons, that's twenty bucks, kid—and that's wholesale! Do you have twenty bucks ready for Lucky the Birthday Clown?"

"I'll have it." Jed hoped he'd have it.

"Then here's my number." Lucky pulled a pink business card from behind Jed's ear. "You call me up and tell me where to meet you. I'll drive out and do all fifty at once. Does that sound fair to you?"

"Very fair," said Jed. He took the card and shook hands, waving to Lucky as he left the Burger'n'Joy. "Thanks, Mr. Clown."

"Oh, one thing, kid," Lucky's voice took on a dangerous tone as he filled the next balloon. "If you call me up, you'd better have the money."

Jed nodded, swallowing hard as he walked out the door into the parking lot. Lucky was not a clown he wanted to mess with.

Later that afternoon, he and Pal found a box of thin rubber gloves in Pal's garage. They made excellent balloons because they inflated really huge, they were strangely shaped, and best of all, they didn't cost anything.

"Listen to this!" Pal brought a small air horn from out of his father's motor home. When he pressed on the top, it howled louder than Jed's brother's stereo system. "My father used it on the freeway to scare people when they drove badly," Pal said. "But then he got a ticket."

"Ideal!" said Jed.

All they needed now was twenty dollars, some alien stuff, and a light to tie onto the balloons. After a long hour's search, Jed found a package of chemical light sticks in his dad's camping gear. They were small plastic tubes that glowed bright yellow when bent in half. "It's the same kind of glow as a firefly," said Jed, reading the directions.

"When you twist the tube, two different chemicals mix. It stays bright for hours!"

One by one, their problems were solved. Jed sold a portable radio to his brother for thirty dollars. Friday morning, Pal raced across the schoolyard with the last bit of good news. "I have the alien remains!" he gasped. Pal wasn't used to running, so Jed had to wait almost five minutes until he caught his breath.

"What do you have?"

"Hold on..." Pal leaned against a wall, wheezing. "My dad took me to the forest yesterday up by the park. I went exploring while he shot his rifle. I found this cabin full of weird blobs of metal and glass. Somebody has a small lab there; we can get all the UFO remains we want. They'll never miss any of it. Best of all, it's on the way to the campgrounds."

"Ideal!" Jed punched Pal in the

stomach playfully. "I have to go now," he said. "Tonight I'll call our clown with the information; then we can pack." As he jogged to his class, Jed felt almost superhuman. With luck, this would be the very last time he would ever see Mr. Bledso. Girls, fame, and adventure would be his. Finally, he was taking charge of his life.

Chapter 3

Everything was ready by Saturday. Lucky met them at the far corner of the campground parking lot, late in the afternoon. One by one he filled the gloves, Jed knotted the ends, and Pal tied them into a bundle. And it was a strangely shaped bundle indeed by the time Lucky filled all fifty. The rubber gloves took on a pale flesh color when they were blown up, and the fingers stuck out at odd angles all over the top. The UFO was almost ten feet long. Pal had a hard time holding it down.

Lucky coughed, snuffed his most recent cigarette out against the door of his pick-up, and took the money. He eyed the floating bundle suspiciously.

"Just what do you plan to do with this, kid?"

"A science experiment," said Pal.

Lucky shook his head. He leaned into Pal's face, with a frightening grin. "What kind of experiment, kid? Quick."

Jed blurted out the first word that came to him. "Baseball ... I mean, weather science—meteorology."

"Right." Lucky climbed into his dusty pink and green truck. He pointed to the load of clown gear in the back. "I've been a clown for two and a half years. I know a prank when I see one." He lit his tenth cigarette of the evening, revved his engine, and gave them both the thumbs up. "Good job, boys." With a loud honk of his horn, Lucky squealed out of the parking lot and disappeared in a cloud of dust.

"Now we can find the alien junk and set up camp," said Jed, putting on his backpack. "Hurry, before the sun goes down."

Pal walked thirty yards ahead of Jed to make sure no one saw the UFO before they launched it. After about fifteen minutes they came to the cabin Pal had found on Thursday. It sat by itself in the woods, with a flat red roof and a pink flamingo lawn ornament out front. "There's nobody home, so we go around back," said Pal. They walked around to a large square shed full of cast iron equipment. Puddles of metal had fallen to the dirt floor and cooled, forming strange round blobs. Pal filled a bag with the metal and tied it to their UFO.

The boys walked north, Pal scouting ahead for campers. There was one group of old Japanese fishermen playing poker in a clearing, but Pal signaled Jed to walk far around them.

As it got dark, Jed became worried that some of the gloves might pop if he brushed against any thorns. "Let's stop here," he called to Pal, about a mile and a half from the fishermen. "Those guys looked out of shape; we can run from them if they're actually brave enough to come look for the UFO."

Jed unpacked as Pal dropped on the ground to rest. "This food I'm carrying is heavier than my dad," he said.

Jed gathered wood, Pal prepared the food, and they cooked and ate and watched the stars. The moon hadn't risen yet, so they could see all of the Milky Way across the sky. "That's our galaxy," said Pal, raising one of his mother's vegetable burgers to his lips. "You know, I wish aliens *would* come and take us away. Life on Earth just isn't everything I want it to be."

"Shut up and eat," said Jed. "You'll need the energy when we have to run tonight. Anyway, it's not a kidnapping if you agree to go with them. We have to put up a fight. Girls like that sort of thing. You want a date with your next-door neighbor, Amy, don't you?"

"Of course. She's the most beautiful girl in the world," said Pal, "except for some people on TV."

"Then there has to be a fight during the kidnapping."

Jed leaned back and watched the stars some more. He was well fed and extraordinarily happy to be far, far away from anything having to do with Astronomy 101—who needed it? After about ten minutes of silently watching the sky, they saw a falling star. It darted down like a brilliant white flame, and then flashed into darkness.

"I think that's our hint," said Jed. He took the bag of metal and tossed the strange round blobs in a circle around them.

Next, he unwrapped two of the light sticks. He bent them in half, shook them up, and they glowed a bright green. "We tie the sticks up in the middle of the UFO so it glows from within," he said. "UFOs have to glow from within."

Pal held the UFO while Jed took the air horn. He had a roll of heavy-duty tape, too. Jed pulled off a long strip and held it ready. "You're all set?" he said. "Once I tape this button down we're doing an illegal act that could have us sent to detention for the rest of the year."

"Hurry! It's yanking my arm off!" said Pal.

"We're going to spend four solid months of fun and excitement at your uncle's cabin."

Pal nodded frantically.

"Good," said Jed. He slapped the tape down over the air horn. In the silence of the forest its high-pitched whine was painful. Jed tied it to one of the light sticks. Then Pal let go.

The UFO rocketed upward. It screamed across the sky. In less than ten seconds it rose howling over the trees—a round, green, frightening blob.

"We better run before the fishermen come." Jed pulled on his backpack and jogged north toward the trail that would take them to Pal's uncle's cabin.

At the edge of the clearing he turned around. Pal stood unmoved, lit by the faint glow of the UFO, with a strange smile on his face.

"It's so beautiful," he said.

"Come on!" Jed ran back and grabbed his friend by the shoulder. "Are you crazy?"

"Look at it," said Pal. The UFO had stopped at about two hundred feet. It hovered directly over them, still screaming. A strange current of air caught the UFO and it began to float east, toward the edge of the park. "I hope," Pal said, "that whoever finds it takes good care of it for us."

"Finds it?" Jed slapped himself on the forehead. "Oh, no! It's going back near the town! If someone finds it, we'll be in detention by the end of the week. You're the idea man; why didn't you figure that out?"

Pal scratched his head. "You didn't tell me to think about the results of our

27

actions. That wasn't part of the plan."

"We'll ditch our packs here and go catch it," said Jed. "People must have seen it already. The air horn won't last for more than a few minutes, will it?"

"It shouldn't," said Pal. "My dad used it all the time until the police stopped him."

They leaned their packs against a rock and ran though the forest, following the UFO. It howled like an air-raid siren, about a hundred and fifty feet up. It bobbed through the air looking as frightening as ever, but it was already slowly lowering in the sky.

"It looks like it's going to come down near the sewage treatment plant," said Pal at the edge of the forest. To their right a bright light cut through the darkness. Someone was trying to shine a spotlight on the UFO from a car dealership in the center of town. Luckily, whoever it was didn't have very good aim. "You run ahead," said Pal, gasping for breath. "I'll catch up."

Jed ran down the grassy hill that sloped to the sewage treatment plant. Part of the UFO came apart and about ten of the gloves separated and flew into the sky.

Jed heard the familiar siren of the volunteer fire department's truck rising over the sound of the UFO. He figured he had fifteen minutes to get the UFO and get out of the way.

Suddenly, the air horn's shriek fizzled out. At the bottom of the long, sloping hill was a flat plain of hard-packed dirt. In the middle of this was a shallow black lake run by the treatment plant. Somehow it made the town's garbage less poisonous, but the lake looked about as dangerous as anything Jed had ever seen.

He stopped to catch his breath for a moment and looked up. The UFO was going to land right in the middle of the lake.

There was no way Jed would ever go swimming in that muck. He had to stop the UFO before it passed over the low fence around the lake. Jed searched his pockets; all he had was a pocket knife.

Jed opened the blade halfway, like a boomerang. He threw it as hard as he could at the center of the UFO. The knife toppled end over end, disappearing into the darkness. And nothing happened.

Suddenly, the UFO seemed to explode. At least fifteen gloves flew off and rose into the air. Then the main body of the thing shook and sank like a rock. Jed was completely out of breath by the time he ran up to it. It lay like a huge, dead jellyfish right at the base of the fence.

Jed untied the last light stick and threw it into the water. It sank through the thick, ugly muck like a radioactive monster in the last scene of an old science-fiction film. He stomped on the rest of the gloves, popping every one of them, as the town's fire truck swerved onto the long dirt road that led to the plant. Jed stuffed the popped gloves into his pants pocket and ran back toward the forest, just as the firemen arrived.

He stumbled into the campsite about thirty minutes later, completely exhausted. Pal was waiting there, eating a candy bar and reading a comic book. "Want a diet soda?"

"I want to sleep," said Jed.

"Too bad for you," Pal laughed. "We have to move camp quick before somebody comes searching. The Channel Five helicopter flew over twice already." He unwrapped a foil-covered cream-filled pastry and offered it to Jed. "We're famous—and it's only eleven-thirty."

Chapter 4

Jed and Pal walked north for another two miles or so, until neither boy could take another step. Then they laid out their sleeping bags, completely exhausted.

When the sun rose the next morning, they crawled out and started walking. They marched up the thin Forest Service path for a few miles, and then left the state park. Finally, at about four-thirty in the afternoon, they came to Kroger's Lake. Pal pointed to a small cabin near the water. There was a huge boulder next to it that would be great for jumping into the lake.

"That's our cabin over there," he said.

"The one with the laundry hanging next to it?" said Jed quietly.

Pal turned and squinted for a better look. There was laundry hanging on the line. There was a strange chugging noise coming from the rear of the cabin, and in the window he could see someone moving around.

"You said no one would be living here!" Jed was very, very tired. "You said all your uncle did was watch TV."

They walked up quietly, hiding behind the boulder near the cabin. "Look," said Pal, pointing around back. "I was right about one thing. My uncle is inside watching TV."

"That doesn't help us," said Jed. "Let's go in closer. Maybe they're ready to go home." The boys set their packs against the boulder and crawled across the ground to the cabin window. It was open and they could hear the sound of the TV inside. Pal's uncle, a large man with a huge belly, sat in a folding lawn

chair. The news was on. His wife was in the kitchen cooking something that smelled like it had been bought from a veterinarian.

Slowly and carefully, they raised their heads over the level of the window sill. Fortunately, Pal's uncle was facing the TV. Unfortunately, on TV was a picture of Pal and Jed. Jed grabbed Pal's shoulder with excitement. The picture changed. An announcer now stood at the edge of the forest. He spoke in very dramatic terms about the UFO and the brave young men who had disappeared. Pal's uncle sat, silently staring straight ahead.

"We're famous!" whispered Jed. "We're minor stars!"

"No," said Pal. "We're busted."

The TV cut to a picture of Professor Bledso from Astronomy 101. Jed gulped. "An expert has been called in on the case," said the announcer. "Professor Edward Bledso, science teacher for Spiro Agnew Junior High School. We spoke to him at his research lab, here in the Nelson Rockefeller Campgrounds." Bledso was standing in front of a cabin in the woods. It was a strange little cabin, with a flat red roof. In the front yard stood a pink flamingo lawn ornament.

"Oh, no!" Jed slapped himself in the forehead. "It was Bledso's cabin! He'll find his own stuff and figure everything out."

In his fear, Jed spoke a little too loud. Without turning his head, Pal's uncle shouted out the window.

"You kids get moving! If you make me get up, there's going to be some big trouble!"

"Right." Jed walked back to the boulder and shrunk to the ground. "We're doomed." Pal went down beside him.

"We're as good as sitting in detention right now," said Jed. "Bledso will find the stuff we took from his shed and nail us to the wall."

"Well, we just have to go and get it before he sees it," said Pal.

"It took us all day to walk here. We're doomed." Jed would return to Astronomy 101 and drift slowly toward mental illness. "We've failed," he said quietly. "And I never even got to go to community college."

"No," Pal grabbed Jed by the arm. "We can leave our packs here. Without all that weight we can make it to the campsite in a few hours. If we hide all of Bledso's stuff, we can be back here before sundown. It can still work."

"What about your uncle?"

"He only gets seven vacation days a year," said Pal. "He's the head chef at the county correctional institution; they need him to serve the prisoners. We'll camp on the other side of the lake until they leave."

Jed stared into his friend's eyes.

There was a new bravery in Pal, a confidence that he'd never shown before. Jed wasn't about to let Pal be more daring than he was. "Okay," he said, "let's do it."

Chapter 5

That night they camped on the far side of the lake. They roasted vegetable patties and stole oranges from the nearby trees, and in the evening Jed and Pal went swimming. Early the next day, they hid their packs in a pile of dry brush. They marched back to their first campground as quickly as they could. With Pal along, this wasn't very quick. Even so, by eleven-thirty Jed was already creeping over the nearest hill, staring down into their old campsite, searching for Professor Bledso.

Everything seemed to be just as they'd left it. The blobs of metal were all around the ground, shining in the sun. Jed began to whistle as he picked up the metal. So what if the authorities didn't find any alien remains, he thought. He and Pal were still on TV. Maybe if he were to promote himself well enough they might want him for commercials. He could advertise tennis shoes—just the thing to wear when you have to run from alien kidnappers! Everything was in perfect order. But then Jed looked up to see Professor Bledso standing not more than ten feet away, dressed in his familiar black suit, with a familiar sour expression on his face.

They were doomed.

"Back so soon?" Bledso mumbled. Pal looked up from where he was collecting metal and groaned.

"We're just doing our part to help preserve the environment," said Jed.

"Give a hoot and don't pollute?" asked Pal hopefully.

"It wouldn't have worked anyway," Bledso said. "I was in my cabin when you walked by with that ridiculous

UFO."

"It was not ridiculous," said Pal. "We were on Channel Five."

"Now, children," Professor Bledso smiled. His thin lips were even uglier when they were happy. "Admit it. You scared the entire town and made everyone in the volunteer fire department get out of bed for nothing ... didn't you?" He laid a thin hand on each of their shoulders. Jed considered running away, but sooner or later he would have to come back. There was nothing he could do but face the awful truth. They were going to have more detention than any student in the history of Spiro Agnew Junior High School.

Mr. Bledso began walking them both back through the woods to his cabin. "Would it help if we said we're sorry?" asked Pal.

"No," said Bledso, "I don't think that would help at all. I think they might even send you both to prison."

"I don't want that on my employment record!" said Jed. "I'll never be able to get work."

Pal just groaned. He pictured himself standing in line at the prison cafeteria, sadly taking a plate of overcooked beef from his uncle, the chef.

Bledso grinned again, with his frightening lizard-like smile. "I don't imagine you'd like prison very much. What happens there to boys like you isn't very much fun." He loosened his grip on their shoulders and stroked his paper-white chin. "That's why I'm not going to turn you in. You're going to go on television and tell the world that you were kidnapped by aliens." Jed stopped and stared. He wondered if the old man was just playing a cruel joke on them before he called in the cops.

"Why would you do that?" said Jed. "You're a teacher."

"I'm a teacher of astronomy," said

Bledso. "Not enough people are interested in astronomy right now; but they will be when they hear about you and the aliens. I think it will make my students pay more attention in class, don't you?"

"Yes, sir," said Pal, nodding very quickly. "I think that's a wonderful idea, sir. We shouldn't tell anyone at all."

They continued walking in silence. Jed moped. The UFO hadn't helped him miss out on a single day of class.

Bledso opened the door to his cabin and ushered them in. He directed Jed's attention to a table in the far corner, stacked with astronomy books. "Before you can make up a good story, you have to know all about the subject." Bledso clasped his hands together eagerly, looking as much like a zombie as anything Jed had ever seen on film.

"Janice!" he yelled, "Bring the boys some carrot juice, would you?"

Jed stared in amazement as a gorgeous, young, dark-haired girl walked in from the kitchen. She smiled. Her braces shone like silver in the dim cabin light. Jed could hardly breathe.

"Have you met my daughter, Janice?" said Bledso. "She'll help you learn everything you need to know." He nudged Jed in the ribs and whispered, "She's a year older than you, but I hear she likes younger men." Bledso coughed, and his voice returned to its usual loud mumble. "I'll be in the shed making a telescope while you three get to know one another. We've got so much to do today, before the aliens release you…"

Jed nodded eagerly. He smiled at Janice, who was busy readjusting a tiny rubber band in the back of her mouth.

Gradually, Astronomy 101 wasn't looking quite as horrible as it had before. The universe, after all, is a very big place; it is enormously big—bigger than any person on his own could ever hope to imagine. Anything that huge must have something going for it.